Silly Goose and Daft Duck Try to Catch a Rainbow

Sally Grindley

Illustrated by Adrian Reynolds

A Pearson Company

"I don't like my nest," said Silly Goose one day.

"It's too brown, and brown is boring."

ATH	
ATM	
BAD	
COL	
DOR	
KIG	
POL	
WAT	

This book belongs to

....

For Jon, Fiona, and Pollyanna – S.G

For Kieran – A.R.

LONDON, NEW YORK, SYDNEY, DELHI, PARIS,
MUNICH and JOHANNESBURG

First published in Great Britain in 2001
by Dorling Kindersley Limited,
9 Henrietta Street, London WC2E 8PS

2 4 6 8 10 9 7 5 3 1

Text copyright © 2001 Sally Grindley
Illustrations copyright © 2001 Adrian Reynolds
The author's and illustrator's moral rights have been asserted.

A CIP catalogue record for this book is available from the British Library.

ISBN 0-7513-3529-0

Colour reproduction by Dot Gradations, UK
Printed in China by South China Press

See our complete
catalogue at
www.dk.com

"Let's find some pretty things to put in it,"
said Daft Duck.

"Ooo," said Silly Goose, "that's a good idea."

So off they went for a walk.

Daft Duck saw a big yellow stone.

"This will look good in your nest," he said.

He tried to lift it, but it was too heavy.

Silly Goose found a red flower. "This will look pretty in my nest," she said. She tucked it under her wing.

"Ooo, it tickles!" she giggled.

Buzz!

Silly Goose gazed at her flower. "It's all **squashed**," she moaned.

Daft Duck quacked excitedly. "Look! There's a blue and pink and orange thing up that tree."

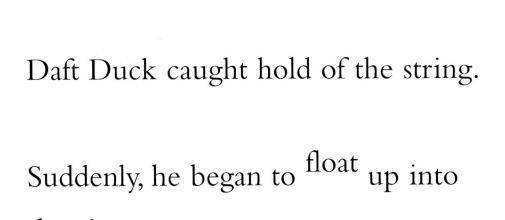

Daft Duck caught hold of the string.

Suddenly, he began to float up into the air...

"Come back!" squawked Silly Goose.

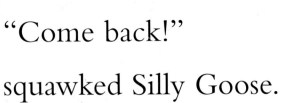

Daft Duck let go.

"Ouch!" yelped Clever Fox.

"Sorry," said Daft Duck.

"Hello, Clever Fox," said Silly Goose. "Will you help us find something colourful for my nest?"

Clever Fox smiled a hungry smile. "Why don't you dig a hole and catch a rainbow?" he said.

"Ooo, that's a good idea," said Silly Goose and Daft Duck.

They began to dig.

While they dug, Clever Fox fetched a great big net.

"Jump into the hole and see if it's deep enough," he said.

Silly Goose and Daft Duck j^u^mp_e_d in.

"Perfect," said Silly Goose.

"Just right," said Daft Duck.

"I'll make sure this net's the right size,"

said Clever Fox.

"Hey, that's my fishing net!"
A great big voice boomed.

Clever Fox turned and
saw Grizzly Bear.

"Just admiring it," he
said, and shot off into
the woods.

"He was going to help us catch a rainbow," grumbled Silly Goose.

"You'll have to help instead," said Daft Duck.

They sat down by the hole...

and waited...

and waited...

Other Toddler Books to collect:

Goodbye, Hello! by Shen Roddie, illustrated by Carol Thompson

Ten in a Bed by Jan Ormerod

My Do It! by Ros Asquith, illustrated by Sam Williams

Ball! by Ros Asquith, illustrated by Sam Williams

Panda Big and Panda Small by Jane Cabrera

Rory and the Lion by Jane Cabrera

Here comes the Rain by Mary Murphy

Caterpillar's Wish by Mary Murphy

You Smell by Mary Murphy

I Feel Happy by Mary Murphy

Baby Loves by Michael Lawrence, illustrated by Adrian Reynolds

Baby Loves Hugs and Kisses by Michael Lawrence, illustrated by Adrian Reynolds

No Bath Tonight! by Harriet Ziefert, illustrated by Emily Bolam

To the Island by Charlotte Agel

Hello Toes! Hello Feet! by Ann Paul, illustrated by Nadine Bernard Westcott

Grumble-Rumble! by Siobhan Dodds

Ting-a-ling! by Siobhan Dodds

The Pig Who Wished by Joyce Dunbar, illustrated by Selina Young

Ned's Rainbow by Melanie Walsh

Hide and Sleep by Melanie Walsh

I'm Too Busy by Helen Stephens

What About Me? by Helen Stephens

Silly Goose and Daft Duck Play Hide-and-Seek by Sally Grindley, illustrated by Adrian Reynol

Grandma Rabbitty's Visit by Barry Smith

One Smiling Sister by Lucy Coats, illustrated by Emily Bolam

Parsnip by Sue Porter

Parsnip and the Pink Blanket by Sue Porter

Parsnip and the Runaway Tractor by Sue Porter

Parsnip and the Sheep Game by Sue Porter